I0601728

Renewed Life Cycle

Table of Contents

Part One: <u>The Trapper</u>

The dawn mist clung to the coastal bush like breath on glass. Dora checked her watch, it read 5:47 AM. She stopped to adjust the weight of her pack. Thirty-two traps to check before lunch.

She'd been doing this work for six years now, ever since the Landcare Group hired her fresh out of conservation training. Back then, she'd been idealistic, eager to save native birds by eliminating introduced predators. Now it was simply her job, a rhythm as natural as breathing.

Her boots crushed the undergrowth as she walked the familiar track. Somewhere above, a tui sang its liquid melody, and she smiled. That's why she did this work, for moments like these, for the chance to hear birdsongs that might otherwise be silenced by rats, stoats, and possums.

The first trap was empty. So was the second. The third held a young brush-tailed possum, still alive, its dark eyes watching her approach.

"Sorry, mate," she murmured, reaching for her dispatch tool. "Nothing personal."

But something stopped her hand. The possum wasn't struggling. It was looking at her, really looking, with an intensity that felt almost human. Its small paws were pressed together, and for one impossible moment, Dora could have sworn it was pleading.

She shook her head. Anthropomorphism. Classic rookie mistake. These were pests, invasive species decimating New Zealand's native ecosystem.

The Department of Conservation's data was clear: possums consumed 21,000 tonnes of native vegetation every night. They spread bovine tuberculosis. They ate eggs and chicks from nests. This was conservation, not cruelty.

The dispatch was quick. Professional. She'd done it thousands of times.

Yet as she recorded the kill in her notebook…Possum #2,847…she felt an unusual heaviness. The morning seemed darker somehow, the birdsong more distant.

By midday, she'd cleared fifteen traps. Seven kills: four rats, two stoats, one more possum. She ate her sandwich overlooking the coast, watching the Tasman Sea fold and unfold against the rocks. Her phone buzzed, a text from Maya, her flatmate and closest friend.

Curry tonight? Got fresh coriander from the market.

Dora smiled and replied with a thumbs up. Simple pleasures. Good people. Meaningful work. Life was good.

The afternoon brought more of the same routine. She reset traps, repositioned lures, made notes about tracks and signs. At trap number twenty-seven, she found a monarch butterfly resting on a flax flower, its orange and black wings slowly opening and closing in the afternoon sun.

Without thinking, focused on extracting a stuck trap pin, she stepped forward. Her boot came down.

The crunch was tiny, barely audible, but it stopped her cold. She lifted her foot and saw the broken wings, the small body twitching in the grass.

"Oh no," she whispered, kneeling down. "I'm so sorry."

It was just a butterfly. Just an accident. But watching it die, she felt a strange pulling sensation behind her eyes, a tightness in her chest she couldn't explain.

She stayed there longer than she should have, watching until the butterfly was completely still.

The evening passed normally. Maya's curry was excellent, fragrant with cumin and cardamom. They watched a documentary about climate change, argued good-naturedly about whether lab-grown meat would ever catch on, and went to bed at reasonable hours.

Dora dreamed of flying.

The next morning started with trap thirty. A large brush-tailed possum, male, caught by the leg. This one was fighting, thrashing against the chain, eyes wild with terror.

"Hey, hey," Dora said softly, approaching slowly. "I'll make it quick. I promise."

But the possum didn't calm down. It screamed, a sound she'd heard before but never quite like this. It sounded almost like words, like someone trying to speak through a throat that couldn't form the sounds.

Please. Please don't. I won't do it again. Please.

Dora froze. The voice was in her head. It had to be. Possums didn't talk.

The animal's eyes locked onto hers, and she saw something there, recognition, intelligence, desperation. Not animal panic but human fear.

"This is ridiculous," she muttered, but her hands were shaking.

She raised the dispatch tool. The possum's eyes never left hers. And in that split second before she struck, she could have sworn she saw understanding. Acceptance. Forgiveness.

The first blow landed with a sickening thud. The possum's body jerked.

Then came the headache.

It was like nothing she'd ever experienced, a spike of white-hot agony that drove through her skull from temple to temple. Dora dropped the tool and clutched her head, collapsing beside the trap, beside the dying possum.

Their eyes met. Both of them, in agony. Both of them, fading.

The world began to glow amber, the edges of her vision blurring into golden light. She tried to speak, tried to move, but her body wouldn't respond. The possum's chest rose and fell one last time, and then…

Nothing.

Part Two: <u>The Possum</u>

Consciousness returned like surfacing from deep water.

Dora opened her eyes, except they weren't her eyes. Everything looked different: colours shifted toward blues and greens, her depth perception was off, and the world seemed both sharper and stranger.

She was still in the bush. Still by the trap.

And there, lying motionless in the grass, was her own body.

"No," she tried to say, but what came out was a chittering sound. "No, no, no…"

She looked down. Fur. Gray-brown fur covered small paws. Her paws.

Panic flooded through her. This wasn't possible. This couldn't be happening. She was dreaming, hallucinating, dying, something…anything but this.

She scrambled away from her own corpse, moving on four legs with a coordination that felt both foreign and instinctive. Her mind was human, but her body knew how to move, how to grip, how to climb.

A distant shout made her freeze. Maya's voice, calling her name.

Dora tried to run toward it, to call back, but her possum body had other ideas. Every instinct screamed *danger* and sent her scurrying up the nearest tree instead. She clung to a branch, watching as Maya appeared on the track below.

'Dora? Dora!"

Maya found the body. Found her. Dora watched her best friend's face crumble, watched her drop to her knees, watched her check for a pulse with shaking hands.

"No, no, no," Maya sobbed. "Please no. Dora, please…"

From the tree, Dora tried to cry out. But all that emerged was a distressed possum call.

Maya looked up, saw her in the branches, and for one wild moment Dora thought she'd been recognized. But Maya just wiped her eyes and pulled out her phone, fingers trembling as she dialed emergency services.

"I'm here," Dora tried to say. "I'm right here. It's me."

But she was a possum. And Maya couldn't hear her at all.

The days that followed were a nightmare of helpless observation. Dora attended her own funeral from the rafters of the crematorium, watching friends and colleagues share memories of someone they'd never see again. Maya spoke, barely holding it together, about losing a sister in all but blood.

Dora wanted to comfort her. Instead, she had to hide from the building's caretaker who tried to shoo her out with a broom.

She visited her own grave at the coastal cemetery, read her own headstone: *Dora Elizabeth Chen, 1990-2025. She walked gently on the earth.*

The irony was bitter enough to taste.

But slowly, impossibly, life began to find new patterns. Possum life was simpler in some ways. Food was where you found it: flowers, leaves, fruits, the occasional insect. Sleep came in drowsy daylight hours, curled in hollow trees. The night came alive with sounds and smells her human senses had never registered.

She learned the territories of other possums, the flight paths of moreporks, the way the wind warned of weather changes hours before they arrived. She witnessed the forest's hidden architecture, who ate what, who hunted whom, the delicate balance humans tried to manage with traps and poison but never fully understood.

Two months passed. Then three.

Dora found herself almost content. Perhaps this was her life now. Perhaps she could make peace with it.

Then came the trap.

She smelled the lure before she saw it, a sweet, irresistible scent that called to something deep in her possum brain. Her human mind recognized it: cinnamon and flour paste, standard DOC 200 bait. she was all too familiar as she had her own special recipe, she liked to call Hansel and Gretel Mix.

"Don't," she told herself. "You know what this is."

But her body was already moving toward it, drawn by instincts stronger than knowledge. She tried to stop, to turn away, but the hunger overrode everything.

Her paw touched the trigger plate.

The trap snapped shut with a sound like breaking bone. Pain exploded through her leg, white, consuming, absolute. She screamed and thrashed, but the trap held fast.

Time became meaningless. There was only pain and panic and the certain knowledge of what came next.

Footsteps on the trail. Human footsteps.

Maya appeared through the trees, and Dora's heart (she had realized, over these months, that possums had remarkably strong hearts) simultaneously leaped with hope and sank with dread.

"Please," she tried to say. "Maya, it's me. It's Dora. Please don't..."

But it came out as distressed chittering.

Maya's face was sad as she approached. Tear tracks still visible on her cheeks, she'd been crying again. The grief hadn't left her.

"I'm sorry," Maya whispered, not to the possum but to the memory of her friend. "I'm doing this for you, Dora. For the work you believed in."

She raised the dispatch tool.

"NO!" Dora screamed. "MAYA, IT'S ME! PLEASE!"

Their eyes met. For one heartbeat, Dora thought she saw recognition flicker there. But then Maya's face hardened with necessity, and the tool came down.

Once. Twice.

The world exploded into amber and golden light, as it had before, then

Darkness.

Part Three: <u>The Butterfly</u>

Awakening was gentler this time. Softer.

Dora became aware of sunlight…real sunlight, not filtered through possum eyes but broken into a thousand fractured rainbows. The world was a kaleidoscope of ultraviolet patterns invisible to humans, flowers glowing with landing strips and nectar guides.

She was tiny. Impossibly light. And when she looked down, she saw six delicate legs, a furled proboscis, and wings that caught the light like stained glass windows.

A monarch butterfly.

Memory rushed back…stepping on a butterfly weeks ago, before everything changed. An accident. A genuine accident. But apparently that didn't matter.

She was experiencing the lives of those she'd harmed. All of them.

Her mind reeled with implications. The possum had been deliberate, executed as part of her work. But how many others? How many rats, stoats, ferrets? How many accidental deaths…spiders crushed, moths caught in closing doors, ants beneath her heel?

Her trap records alone numbered in the thousands.

Would she live with each one? Decade after decade of brief, terrified lives, ending in death again and again and again?

The thought was too large to hold. She landed on a kowhai flower and drank nectar with a tongue she didn't know how to use but somehow did. The sweetness was transcendent, more complex than any human food she remembered.

She had to focus on now. In this life,
however brief. On not causing more harm
that would need to be repaid.

The butterfly's instincts were different from
the possum's, more about flight patterns
and temperature regulation than territory
and food storage. But beneath it, she felt
something else. Memories that weren't
hers. A butterfly's brief life: emerging from
a chrysalis, the first flight, finding this very
flower.

Had there been another consciousness
here before her? Another soul displaced by
her arrival, moving on to... what?

She thought of the possum she'd
inhabited. Whose life had she interrupted?
Where had that original consciousness
gone?

The questions spiraled into terrifying
implications about the nature of existence,
the chain of being, the cosmic ledger of
cause and effect.

A shadow passed overhead. Dora looked up to see a fantail darting through the air, a native bird, beautiful, protected by law.

Also a predator of butterflies.

She took flight instinctively, wings catching air in ways that felt like dancing. But the fantail was fast, evolved for exactly this kind of chase.

Dora zigged and zagged, flew high then low, but the bird stayed close. In her peripheral vision (which was remarkably wide in a butterfly) she saw it closing in...

And then, impossibly, she saw herself.

Human Dora, trudging up the trail, burdened with her usual pack of traps and tools. Younger-looking, healthier, from before... before everything.

This was impossible. This was...

A time loop? A parallel timeline? A vision?

Butterfly-Dora flew directly at her human self, desperate to warn her, to communicate, to somehow break this cycle.

Human-Dora looked up, surprised by the butterfly's aggressive flight pattern. She stumbled back...

And swatted.

It was defensive, instinctive. But Dora felt her wing crumple, her small body spinning out of control. She crashed into the grass, legs twitching uselessly.

Above her, human-Dora knelt down, stricken.

"Oh no," her own voice said. "A monarch. I'm so sorry, little one."

She watched herself watching her die. The irony would have been funny if it weren't so devastating.

The amber light came again, and Dora
wondered what fresh horror waited in the
darkness.

But something was different this time.

Part Four: <u>The Awakening</u>

The alarm clock blared at 5:30 AM, same as always.

Dora sat bolt upright in bed, gasping, her heart hammering against ribs that felt impossibly large and familiar. Human ribs. Human heart.

She was human again.

Her hands...her actual hands...shook as she felt her face, her arms, her legs. All there. All human. All alive.

'Oh my god," she whispered. "Oh my god."

The smell of burning toast drifted from the kitchen. Maya, making breakfast. Maya, who was alive. Who hadn't found her body in the bush.

Dora stumbled out of bed and ran to the kitchen, grabbing Maya in a fierce hug that made her flatmate yelp with surprise.

"Whoa! Good morning to you too! Bad dream?"

"Something like that," Dora said, voice muffled against Maya's shoulder. "How long have I been asleep?"

"Uh, the usual amount? It's Tuesday. You okay?"

Tuesday. The same Tuesday she'd started her rounds. The same Tuesday it had all begun.

Over burnt toast and salvaged jam, Dora tried to explain her dream…the trap, the death, becoming a possum, then a butterfly. Maya listened with the patient expression of someone who'd heard weirder things before from Dora…

"That's intense," Maya said. "But you know dreams are weird. Your brain processes stuff symbolically. You probably just need a vacation."

Dora wanted to believe that. She desperately wanted to believe that.

But when they set out on the morning trap line, everything felt too familiar. Too exact. The same mist, the same bird calls, the same path.

She checked trap after trap with her heart in her throat, dreading what she'd find.

Trap thirty was empty.

Relief flooded through her…until she rounded the next bend and saw it: a monarch butterfly on a kowhai flower, surrounded by native grass, newly emerged and testing its wings in the morning sun.

Dora stopped breathing.

The butterfly lifted off and began to circle her. Spiraling closer, its flight pattern deliberate, purposeful.

Not random.

Not instinctive.

She stood perfectly still as it landed on her outstretched hand, its tiny feet tickling her palm.

"Dora?" Maya called from up ahead. "You coming?"

The butterfly's wings opened and closed slowly. Dora looked into its compound eyes and saw…

Everything.

Not memory, exactly. Not vision. But understanding.

She saw the web of life in all its terrifying complexity. Every creature connected, every action rippling outward through space and time.

She saw her own kills replayed not with judgment but with consequence: The rat pup that starved when she trapped its mother rat, the stoat's kits that died alone in their den, the possum that would have lived another five years if not for her trap.

But she also saw the native birds she'd saved. The kokako chicks that fledged because rats were controlled. The dotterel nests that survived because stoats were removed. The forest slowly recovered, canopy by canopy.

She saw karma not as punishment but as learning. As walking in another's skin until you truly understood what it meant to live and die, to fear and hope, to be someone other than yourself.

The butterfly lifted off her palm and flew a lazy circle around her head.

Then it flew to Maya.

It landed on her friend's shoulder, and Maya laughed with delight. "Oh wow, look! It's so beautiful!"

The butterfly crawled down Maya's arm, across her hand, and took flight again…heading back down the trail, away from the traps.

Dora watched it disappear into the morning light and understood.

This was not a dream. This was not a warning.

This was a gift.

She finished the trap line that day, but everything had changed. At each trap, she paused. She really looked at what she'd caught, acknowledged the life that had ended, whispered apologies and gratitude for their sacrifice in service of the larger ecosystem.

At trap thirty, she found another possum. But this time she saw the individual, not just the pest. A young female, probably her first breeding season. Dora made the dispatch as humane as possible, then sat with the body for a moment, hand on its soft fur.

'I'm sorry," she said. "I know you were someone too. Thank you for your life. I won't waste what you've given."

Maya gave her a strange look when she caught up, but said nothing.

That evening, Dora sat at her laptop and began writing. Not a report, not a conservation plan, but a story about a woman who had to learn compassion the hardest way possible.

She wrote about walking in another's skin. About the intricate web that connected all living things. About finding balance between protection and harm, between necessary action and mindless cruelty.

She wrote until her fingers ached and her eyes burned.

And when she finally slept, she dreamed of flying again. But this time, she remembered the joy in it.

The End.

Epilogue: <u>The Great Unknown</u>

Six months later, Dora stood at the same coastal lookout, watching the Tasman Sea fold and unfold against ancient rocks. She still worked for the Landcare Group, still ran trap lines and still dispatched invasive species.

But everything had changed.

She'd advocated for and implemented new protocols: quicker kill times, strategic rather than blanket trapping, careful documentation of every animal taken. She started education programs for local schools, teaching children about interconnectedness, about making hard choices with open eyes.

She'd adopted a saying from indigenous Māori practice: *Kia Tupato* – be careful, be mindful.

Before each trap check, she whispered it like a prayer.

The organization published her paper on ethical pest control, and she received both praise and criticism. Some called her soft. Some said she'd lost her nerve. But others, conservationists, biologists, even philosophers, reached out to say she'd articulated something they'd long felt but couldn't express.

Maya noticed the change most of all.

"You're different," she said one evening over dinner. "Gentler, somehow. But also... clearer. Like you know something the rest of us don't."

Dora smiled. "Maybe I do. Or maybe I just finally understood something I should have known all along."

"Which is?"

"That we're all connected. All the same consciousness wearing different bodies.

And every time we take a life…even necessarily, even righteously…we're killing a version of ourselves."

Maya was quiet for a long moment. Then: "That butterfly really got to you, didn't it?"

"Yeah," Dora said. "It really did."

She still saw monarchs sometimes, dancing through the coastal bush. She'd stop and watch them, these fragile creatures that lived only weeks but blazed with such vivid beauty.

She wondered if any of them carried human memories. Wondered if consciousness truly cycled through forms, learning and growing with each iteration.

She didn't know. No one did. That was the beautiful terror of existence…the great unknown that wrapped around all certainties like darkness around stars.

But she'd learned to walk more gently on the earth. To see the individual in every creature. To acknowledge the weight of every death, even those she couldn't avoid.

She'd learned that conservation wasn't just about ecosystems…it was about compassion. About recognizing that every being, from possum to person, experienced the world as vividly and urgently as she did.

She'd learned that we are all, in the end, renewed through the cycle of life. Born and reborn, learning and forgetting and learning again.

And she'd learned the most important lesson of all: that empathy isn't weakness.

It's remembering we're all made of the same stardust, all pilgrims on the same journey, all trying to survive in bodies we didn't choose, but must honor while we have them.

On her desk, she kept a small frame with two reminders:

Walk gently.

Every life matters.

And whenever she went out to check her traps, she carried the memory of wings…light as air, bright as hope, brief as a heartbeat.

For the possums, the butterflies, and all the lives we touch without meaning to. May we learn to see with more than our eyes, to feel with more than our hands, and to understand that we are all connected in ways we're only beginning to comprehend.

In the cycle of life and death, in the space between breaths, we are all one consciousness experiencing itself subjectively.

Walk gently. Every moment is precious.

Every life is someone.

<u>Author's Note</u>:

This story is about karma, but not in the simplistic sense of cosmic punishment. It's about empathy. The deep, transformative kind that only comes from truly inhabiting another's perspective.

New Zealand's conservation efforts are real and necessary. Introduced species like possums, rats, and stoats devastate native ecosystems that evolved without mammalian predators. The work of trappers and conservationists saves endemic species from extinction.

But this story asks: can we do necessary harm with open eyes and open hearts? Can we acknowledge the consciousness in every creature, even those we must kill? Can we hold both truths, that individual lives matter AND that ecosystems matter, without collapsing into paralysis?

The universe is more mysterious than we can comprehend. Perhaps consciousness does cycle through forms. Perhaps we've all been everything, at some point in the vast spiral of time. Perhaps the separation we perceive between self and other is the grandest illusion of all.

Or perhaps not. Perhaps this is just a story.

But either way, the lesson remains: Walk gently. See clearly. Harm as little as possible. And when harm is necessary, meet it with consciousness, gratitude, and grief.

We are all stardust. We are all connected.

We are all, in the end, in this together.

The extinction rate on Earth is 1,000 to 10,000 times higher than the natural background rate. Species are disappearing before we even discover them. Every action matters. Every life matters.

Choose compassion when you can.

And when you can't…remember.

<u>Author's Second Note</u>:

This book has lived in my mind for decades. Not as words on a page, but as a question that wouldn't let me go: *What if we could truly understand what it means to be another living being?*

I didn't set out to write a story about punishment or judgment. I set out to explore empathy in its most radical form, the kind that comes from literally inhabiting another's existence, feeling their fear, their pain, their desperate will to live. The kind that transforms not just how we think, but how we act in the world.

This story is about karma, yes, but not as cosmic retribution. It's about the interconnectedness of all consciousness, the possibility that the boundaries we perceive between "self" and "other" are far more permeable than we imagine. That perhaps we have all been everything, in the vast cycle of existence. That the spider you crush, the possum in the trap, the butterfly beneath your boot, they are all experiencing reality as vividly and urgently as you are in this moment.

On Conservation and Conscience:

New Zealand's conservation work is vital and necessary. I want to be clear about this. Introduced species like possums, rats, and stoats are devastating native ecosystems that evolved without mammalian predators. The work of trappers, conservationists, and landcare groups is saving endemic species from extinction. This story does not condemn that work.

But what if we could do necessary harm with open eyes and open hearts? What if we could acknowledge the individual life even as we act for the greater ecosystem? This isn't about paralysis or inaction, it's about conscious action. It's about the difference between mindless killing and mindful necessity.

Dora's journey isn't about stopping conservation work. It's about transforming *how* she does it! With gratitude, with grief, with full awareness of the weight of each death. With protocols that minimize suffering. With education that helps others understand these complex choices.

The Deeper Purpose:

I've carried this story for so long because I believe, deeply, urgently…that we need to expand our circle of compassion. Not in a way that makes us helpless, but in a way that makes us more conscious.

Every day, humans make choices that affect other living beings. Some of these choices are necessary. Some are careless. Some are cruel. And most happen without any real awareness of the consciousness on the other side of our actions.

This book asks you to pause. To see. To remember that every creature you encounter is someone, not something.

That they have their own experience of existence, their own will to survive, their own brief moment in the sun.

<u>If This Book Saves One Life</u>:

If even one person reads this and:

- Checks for animals before closing a door
- Moves a spider outside instead of crushing it
- Trap humanely when trapping is necessary
- Questions whether a death is truly unavoidable
- Teaches a child to respect all forms of life
- See a possum, a rat, a butterfly as a conscious being rather than a pest or decoration
- Walk more gently on the earth

...then decades of thinking, dreaming, and hoping will have been worth it.

On the Great Unknown:

We don't know what consciousness is. We don't know if it cycles through forms. We don't know if there's karma, reincarnation, or simply the void. Science can't yet answer these questions, and perhaps it never will.

But we do know this: we share this planet with millions of other species. We're all made of the same atoms that were forged in dying stars billions of years ago. We all respond to pain, seek pleasure, fight for survival, and fear death. In the ways that matter most, we are fundamentally the same.

The Crisis We Face:

The extinction rate on Earth is now 1,000 to 10,000 times higher than the natural background rate. We are in the midst of the sixth mass extinction, and this time, humans are the cause. Species are disappearing before we even discover them. Entire ecosystems are collapsing.

This isn't just about animals…it's about the web of life that sustains us all. When we harm other beings thoughtlessly, when we disrupt ecosystems carelessly, we are ultimately harming ourselves.

But there is still time. There is still hope. If we can learn to see with more than our eyes, to feel with more than our hands, to understand that we are all connected in ways we're only beginning to comprehend…we might yet save what remains!

RENEWED LIFE CYCLE

A Tale of Empathy, Karma, and Redemption

In the cycle of life and death, we are all connected

FREDERICK BARNES